William Shakespeare's

The

WINTER'S TALE

retold by Bruce Coville

illustrated by LeUyen Pham

Dial Books for Young Readers

For Natalie Babbitt
—B.C.

To Gayle Goldstick and Katherine Konoski,
who showed me the way of the Bard . . .
—L.P.

A Note from the Author

"A sad tale's best for winter," says the doomed prince Mamillius in the early part of *The Winter's Tale*. Yet in the end the story is anything but sad. Reversing the course of a tragedy like *Romeo and Juliet*, it moves from darkness to light, with a final scene that holds perhaps the most delicious surprise ending in all of Shakespeare.

The play, being neither comedy nor tragedy, is classified by some scholars as a "romance." It is one of Shakespeare's last, from the same period that gave us *The Tempest*, and though *The Winter's Tale* features none of the magical elements of that play, it still has the *feel* of a fairy tale. With its raging king, rebellious prince, disguised princess, and delightful final scene, it is a particularly good one for young audiences.

That a play approaching its four hundredth birthday can still fascinate, still delight, still move us is testament to both the power of the story it has to tell—and the language with which it tells it.

Though Shakespeare is not nearly as hard to understand as the culture has made him out to be—he did, after all, write for the masses as well as the elite—time has had its way with the language. For this reason a picture book guide to the story is useful for a youngster—or adult!—trying to find his or her way into the world of these plays, so rich and strange and filled with joyous language. Which is why this book, as with the others in this series, is meant as a companion to the play, and in no way intended to be a replacement. What we hope to offer here is a sense of the wonders to be found not only in this play, but in all of the bard's work. This is merely a sampler of the greater joys to be discovered when the time comes to read the work itself, or better yet, see it on the stage.

There is a disease that can twist men's hearts and make them mad, and the name of that disease is jealousy.

This was the sickness that came upon Leontes, King of Sicilia, in what should have been the time of his greatest happiness. He had a lovely and loving wife. He had a fine young son. And his greatest friend, King Polixenes of Bohemia, had been in court for an extended visit.

The jealousy started on the day Polixenes wished to return home. Though Leontes bid him stay, as he had several times before, Polixenes was firm. "I must return to my own kingdom, my own wife and child," he protested.

"*You* speak to him," said Leontes to his queen, Hermione.

This she did, and with loving kindness, for she cherished Polixenes as a friend. But when the visiting king yielded to her request, Leontes saw in it something deeper and darker.

"He would not stay when I asked," Leontes brooded, "yet he so quickly gave way to my wife."

In short order he convinced himself that the two were in love, and had betrayed him.

How Leontes' heart turned and twisted with the pain of this thought. Seeking solace, he called his son, Mamillius, to him. Yet despite the king's love for the boy, the very sight of him made Leontes think all the more of the queen—which only made his pangs of jealousy worse. "Go play, my son," he muttered at last. "Thy mother plays, and I play too, but so disgraced a part it will hiss me to my grave."

As the puzzled prince ran off, the king turned to his trusted advisor Camillo and said, "The queen is untrue."

"You never spoke what did become you less," protested Camillo, who knew the queen to be good and honest.

"Do you not see how they whisper, and lean cheek to cheek, and meet nose to nose? How their laughter stops with a sigh, how they skulk in corners? Is this nothing?"

"My lord, be cured of this diseased opinion!"

"It is true!" insisted Leontes. And when Camillo still resisted he cried, "You lie, you lie! I hate thee, pronounce thee a gross lout, a mindless slave."

Now Camillo saw that jealousy had made the king mad. But there was worse to come, for Leontes next ordered Camillo to poison Polixenes.

This Camillo promised to do, but only to buy time. Instead, he secretly told Polixenes of the danger. They decided to flee the city. Since Polixenes' ships had long been ready to leave, and since Camillo was known and trusted by all the gatekeepers, this they did in speed and safety.

Camillo had hoped that by removing the source of the king's jealousy he might ease that troubled heart. But in this he was mistaken, for Leontes took their flight as proof of his suspicions. With Polixenes gone, he turned all his wrath upon the queen.

Hermione, unaware of the tempest raging in her husband's heart, was in the gardens with her ladies. The young prince had come to visit and the ladies were teasing him about the fact that he would soon have a younger brother or sister, for the queen was heavy with child.

Calling the prince to her side, Hermione said, "Pray, sit by me and tell me a tale."

"Merry or sad?" asked Mamillius.

"As merry as you will," said the queen.

"A sad tale's best for winter," he replied. "I have one of goblins and sprites. I will tell it softly. Yond crickets shall not hear it."

The prince's eyes danced as he lowered his voice to spin his spooky yarn. But before he could say ten words his father stormed in. Snatching Mamillius from Hermione's side, the king roared, "Bear the boy hence. He shall not be near her longer."

"What is this?" cried Hermione.

"You are untrue!" cried the king. And though Hermione protested, and spoke her love, he ordered her taken to prison, claiming she and Polixenes had plotted against his life.

"Do not weep," Hermione told her ladies. "There is no cause, for I am innocent. When you know I deserve prison, that will be the time for tears." Turning to her husband, she said with great dignity, "I never wished to see you sorry. Now I trust I shall."

Several of the lords who had come with Leontes begged him to repent, but their words, instead of calming him, only added to his rage.

"You smell this business with a sense as cold as is a dead man's nose!" he cried. "But I do see it, and feel it. To prove it to you, and the foolish people as well, I have sent two lords to ask the oracle at Apollo's temple. Then we shall know the truth."

While the king ranted, Paulina, wife of lord Antigonus, went to the prison to see Hermione. Though the guard would not let her in, he did allow one of the queen's ladies to come out to speak to her.

From this lady Paulina learned that the queen had been so shaken by what happened that she had been brought early to childbed, and given birth to a little girl.

"If she will trust me with the babe," said Paulina, "I will take it to the king. We do not know how he may soften at the sight of the child."

"The queen had but today told me her wish that someone might do just this for her," said the lady. "And there is no one living so right for this great task."

As for King Leontes, he had one more burden to add to his woes. Prince Mamillius, stricken with sorrow at his mother's shameful treatment, was now unable to eat or sleep, and had begun to waste away. So Leontes was in no mood to hear reason when Paulina burst into the court with the babe in her arms.

"You must not enter!" cried one of the lords.

"Fear you his tyrannous passion more than the queen's life?" asked Paulina as she swept past him.

Her husband, Antigonus, stepped forward to quiet her. But Paulina would not be stopped. "Good liege, I am your most loyal servant, your physician, your obedient counselor, more daring than those who tiptoe around your wrath. I come from the queen"

"Drive this woman hence!" ordered Leontes.

"Let him that values not his eyes first touch me!" cried Paulina, curving her fingers dangerously. "On my own I'll go, but first I'll do my errand. My lord, the good queen—for she *is* good—hath brought you forth a daughter."

Then she laid the infant girl before him.

"This brat is none of mine," raged the king. "Send it to the fire!"

"It *is* yours," said Paulina, fearless in the face of his anger. Then she held up the babe and detailed for the court all the ways in which it resembled its father.

"Treasonous hag!" cried Leontes. "And you, Antigonus, are worthy to be hanged if you will not stay your wife's tongue."

"Hang all the husbands that cannot do that feat and you'll leave yourself hardly one subject," muttered Antigonus.

"Look to the babe, my lord!" cried Paulina as she was at last pushed from the court. "It is *yours!*"

Leontes turned to Antigonus. "You set your wife to this."

"I did not, sir," said Antigonus, and in this the other lords confirmed him.

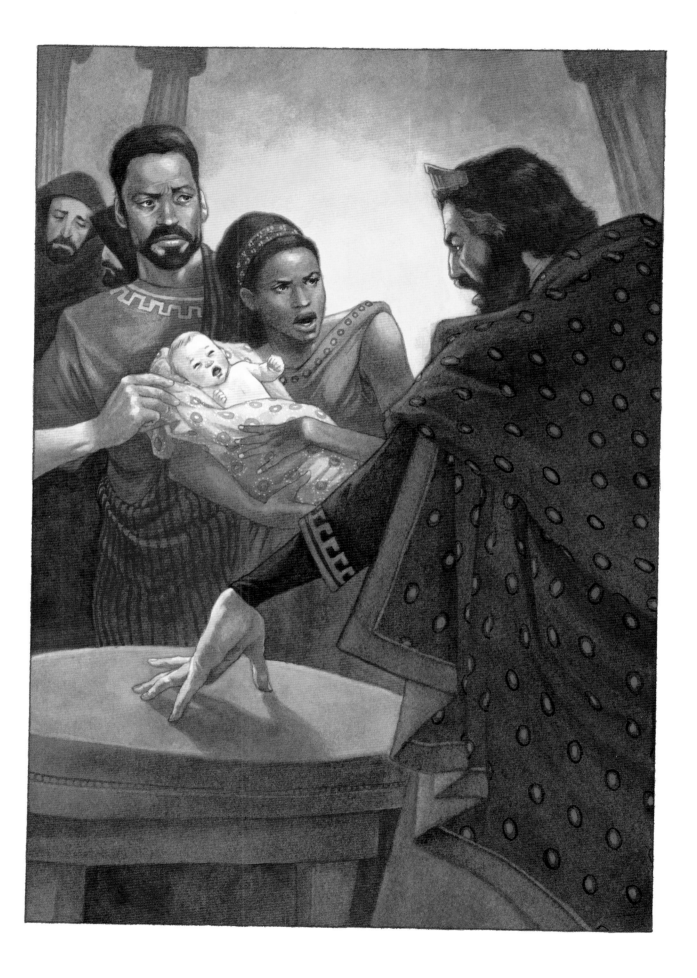

"You're liars all!" raged the king. But as they continued to plead with him, and pledge their loyalty, he calmed. "Antigonus," he said at last, "what will you adventure to save this brat's life?"

"Anything, my lord, that my ability may undergo."

Then Leontes passed this judgment: Antigonus must take the child to some remote place and abandon it, so that fortune might do what it would, whether nurse the child, or end its life.

"I shall do as you order," said Antigonus with heavy heart, "though a present death had been more merciful." And taking up the babe, he left the court.

So intent was Leontes on proving his queen's guilt that he ordered her trial to begin at once. Hermione was brought before the assembled lords, where an officer read the charges.

The queen kept her dignity, and spoke eloquently of her love and fidelity. But the king was unmoved, and pronounced a death sentence.

At this moment the messengers from the oracle arrived. Leontes, convinced that everyone would finally see the truth that had been so obvious to him all along, eagerly had them swear that the sealed message they carried had never been opened since they left Apollo's cave.

"This we swear," they said.

"Then break the seals and read!" ordered the king.

And this is what they read: "Hermione is chaste, Polixenes blameless, Camillo a true subject, Leontes a jealous tyrant, his innocent babe truly begotten; and the king shall live without an heir if that which is lost be not found."

For an instant, Hermione felt as if her life had been given back to her. But the king, still trapped in his jealousy, bellowed, "There is no truth to the oracle! This is mere falsehood."

No sooner had the words left his lips than a servant raced in crying, "My lord, my lord! The prince, your son, with fear of the queen's fate, is gone."

"Gone?" asked Leontes, confused.

"The boy has died of grief," said the woeful man.

In that dreadful moment Leontes realized what a fool he had been. Dropping to his knees he moaned, "Apollo is angry! The heavens themselves strike at my injustice."

"Look!" cried Paulina. "The news is mortal to the queen!"

At her words all turned, and saw that Hermione had crumpled to the floor.

"Take her hence," ordered Leontes. "Her heart is overburdened, but she will recover. I beseech you, tenderly apply some remedies for life."

As they carried his queen away, Leontes lifted beseeching hands to the sky. "Apollo, pardon my great profaneness against thine oracle! I will reconcile myself to Polixenes, new woo my queen, recall the good Camillo." He went on and on with his promises of penitence, admitting his shame and error. But before he could finish, worse news arrived: Paulina entered with a great cry of woe to tell him that the queen was dead.

Many miles and many days away, Antigonus landed on the coast of
Bohemia with the innocent babe. Though Leontes had instructed him
to leave the child in an unknown place, the lord had been haunted by
nightmares in which Hermione appeared and spoke. "As fate has made
you thrower out of my babe, against thy better disposition," said she,
"you will find places remote enough in Bohemia. There weep and leave
it crying. And as the babe is counted lost forever, call it Perdita."

The skies were dark with storm as Antigonus laid down the babe,
along with some small treasures. He was pinning a note to its blanket
when he heard a savage roar. Looking up, he spied a great bear lurching
toward him. With a cry of terror, he raced back toward the ship, the
bear hard on his heels.

Soon after, a humble shepherd came upon the abandoned child, and took it up. As he did, his son came racing to his side and gasped, "I have seen two horrible sights, one at sea, and one on land."

"What sights were these?" asked the shepherd.

"At sea a ship, tossed by a sudden storm, heaving to and fro. And as the sea swallowed it, nearby, on land, I heard the piteous cries of a man being eaten by a bear."

"You met with things dying," said the shepherd, cradling the babe, "I with things newborn. Here's a sight for thee. And look—there's a bundle left with the child. Open it, see what's within."

To the amazement of both men, it was filled with gold.

Thus did Perdita, which means the lost one, come to the coast of Bohemia, and thus were lost all those who knew the secret of her birth. And thus did the shepherd take her home to raise her as his own daughter.

ime passed, as it always will. And as sixteen years flowed by, the shepherd—using some of the gold, but always saving most aside for the child—grew prosperous indeed.

As for Perdita's real father, he too grew with time—grew remorseful of his jealous rage, and ever more aware of what treasures of the heart his foolishness had cost him.

Good Camillo, who had risked his life and fortune to save King Polixenes, had also grown—grown in the favor of Polixenes, grown in wealth, and above all grown in his desire to return to his home-land of Sicilia, which he had not seen in all this time. But to this desire Polixenes would not consent, for he felt a need of Camillo's counsel.

"I require your help with Prince Florizel. He is much absent from the palace, and seldom away from the home of a shepherd—one who, the people say, has risen from modest means to great wealth."

"I have heard of this man," said Camillo. "They say his daughter is a rare gem."

"I fear she is the hook that holds the prince," said the king. "Come, be my partner in this. We must disguise ourselves and discover my son's situation."

The young woman they spoke of was, of course, Perdita, who had grown into a maiden of astonishing beauty. Prince Florizel had spotted her one day when out hunting and—taken with her beauty—had come a-courting. Now they were madly in love, a love they both knew would be forbidden by King Polixenes, who could not let his son marry a mere commoner, as all assumed Perdita to be.

Though Perdita fretted about this, Florizel reassured her. "I'll be thine, my fair, or not my father's. For I cannot be mine own, nor anything to any, if I be not thine."

He spoke these words as they were preparing for the great party that her shepherd father was hosting to celebrate the sheep-shearing. Oddly, though Perdita was dressed like a princess in her festal garb, Florizel had disguised himself—as he always did when he came to visit—to seem a mere peasant.

Before the prince could steal a kiss, the old shepherd scurried up, urging Perdita to take her place as head of the feast. With him came two strangers: Camillo and Polixenes, so carefully disguised that Florizel did not recognize his own father.

Perdita welcomed them graciously, and offered them flowers, as she did all the guests. Her manner and words were so delightful, they moved Florizel to speak much in her praise.

Drawing Camillo aside, the king murmured, "This is the prettiest lass that ever ran on the greensward. Nothing she does but smacks of something greater than herself, too noble for this place."

"She is the queen of curds and cream," agreed Camillo.

The party erupted with new gaiety as a servant rushed in to announce the arrival of a peddler selling songs and ballads, and ribbons in all the colors of the rainbow. The peddler was, in truth, a rogue named Autolycus, who had once worked for the prince but was now in disgrace, and intended to pick the pockets of anyone he could.

As King Polixenes watched the party he grew more and more disturbed, for it was clear that his son was too much in love with the shepherd girl. Deciding to test the boy, he asked Florizel why he did not buy some of the peddler's wares for his fair maiden.

"She prizes not such trifles as these are," said Florizel. "The gifts she seeks from me are in my heart." Then, in his excitement of love, he offered his hand in marriage to Perdita.

The king was appalled. "Have you a father?" he asked.

"I have, but what of him?" replied Florizel, with foolish boldness.

"Knows he of this?"

"He neither does, nor shall."

"Methinks a father is at the nuptial of his son a guest that best becomes the table," fumed Polixenes. "Is he grown stupid? Can he speak? Hear? Know man from man?"

"He has better strength and health than most his age."

"By my beard, you offer him a great wrong not to tell him of your plans!"

"For reasons, my grave sir, which are not fit you know, I do not tell my father of this business."

"Prithee, let him know."

"I shall not!"

"Then mark you your divorce!" cried the king angrily, tearing off his false beard, and with it the rest of his disguise. In his fury he pronounced death on Perdita's father, and condemned Perdita herself to never see the prince again. Then he stormed away, ordering Florizel to follow.

"O sir, you have undone an old man, who thought now only to die in peace," said Perdita's shepherd father, who already seemed to feel the hangman's noose about his neck.

Perdita urged the prince to do as his father commanded. "As for me, I'll queen it no inch farther," she said. "But milk my ewes and weep."

But Florizel was unmoved. "I am sorry, but not afeard," he said, taking her hands. "Delayed, but nothing altered. You are more to me than throne or crown. Let my father wipe me from the succession."

"This is desperate, sir," said Camillo, who had now also removed his disguise.

"So call it, but it fulfills my vow. Not for all Bohemia will I break my oath to my fair beloved. You have been my father's honored friend. I beseech you: When he shall miss me—as he shall, for I mean not to see him anymore—tell him I have put to sea. Where I mean to sail you need not know."

Suddenly Camillo, who loved the prince and the king equally, but also longed for his home in Sicilia, saw a way he might serve them both, and gain his own desire as well.

"If you insist on this flight, then make for Sicilia. Present yourself before the king, and claim your shepherd girl is your princess. I know Leontes. Seeking the forgiveness from you he longs for from your father, he will welcome you in."

"But what cause shall I give for my visit?"

"Tell him you are sent by your father to greet him and give him comfort. I will write all the things you need to know. This is a course far better than abandoning yourselves to unpathed waters, undreamed shores, and certain misery."

Florizel, who was still disguised as a shepherd, realized another problem. "I cannot return home for fresh clothing—nor can I present myself as a prince while dressed in garb such as this!"

Camillo again had an answer. "You know that Leontes, repenting his wrath, has held my land and my fortune in trust. I will give you letters to those who hold it. Stop there first."

As they made their plans, Autolycus—fresh from the feast and filled with self-delight at all the pockets he had picked—came upon them. Spotting the rogue, Camillo saw yet another opportunity, and insisted that the shabby peddler exchange clothes with Florizel. He even paid Autolycus for the exchange, though the rogue was already getting much the better for the trade. The peddler's hat Camillo placed on Perdita's head, telling her to muffle her face.

Once the lovers were properly disguised, the advisor bid them make haste for Florizel's ship. Then he hurried off to carry out a part of his plan he had not revealed to them: He would tell Florizel's father where the youth had fled. He knew Polixenes would follow, and in this way Camillo hoped to reconcile the two kings—and at the same time to bring himself back home.

At least, that is the way it would work if nothing went wrong.

Autolycus, sensing mischief in the air, wanted to be a part of it. He spotted his chance when Perdita's shepherd father and brother appeared. They were on their way to show Polixenes the bundle that had been with Perdita when the shepherd found her. In this way they hoped to prove she was none of the shepherd's blood—and that therefore the shepherd should not be punished for her boldness with the prince. With just a bit of smooth talking Autolycus had them convinced that he was the one to present them to the king, and that their lives depended on him doing so.

But his real plan was to get them onto the king's ship. And, strange to say, in this one thing Autolycus was actually hoping to do a bit of good for the prince, of whom he was still fond. (Which is not to say that he didn't hope to gain something out of it himself as well!)

In Sicilia the court was dark with gloom. The king had not remarried, and, as the prophecy proclaimed, had no heir. To make things worse, Paulina—who the king now deferred to, since she was the only one who had had the courage to speak against the madness of his jealousy—had managed to wrest from him a promise that he would not wed again without her permission. Nor would she let him forget the wrongs he had done while he was in his rage, but ever brought the image of the innocent queen back to his mind.

"Unless another, as like Hermione as is her picture, do come before you, there shall be no second marriage," she said sternly.

As they were debating this, word came that Prince Florizel of Bohemia had arrived, bringing with him the fairest princess in the world. And though Paulina chided the messenger not to forget the beauty of Queen Hermione, it seemed his words were proven true when Florizel and Perdita were ushered in to see the king.

As for Florizel, he looked so like his father in his youth that Leontes was deeply moved and felt again all that he had lost by driving his friend away. But even as he was vowing to make up to the son the wrong he had done the father, another messenger entered to announce that the King of Bohemia himself had now arrived!

Florizel and Perdita felt their hopes crumble. Now her identity as a mere shepherd girl must be revealed. Still, Florizel urged her to be strong. "Though Fortune, visible an enemy, should chase us with my father, power no jot has she to change our loves." Then he begged King Leontes to speak on their behalf.

Leontes agreed to do so. But his help was not needed, for the truth of Perdita's birth was also about to be revealed. Her shepherd father—who had been seasick for the entire voyage and thus had not been able to display the secret he carried—now opened the bundle before both kings. To the astonishment of all, Perdita was proved to be none other than King Leontes' lost daughter.

What joyous weeping, what sorrow-laden laughter followed this discovery, as all delighted in the reunion, yet mourned the time lost, and even more the queen who had died.

Now Paulina offered one last favor. "I have had made a statue of Hermione, by the great Italian sculptor Guilio Romano. Would you, Princess, care to see the likeness of your mother?"

"I would give much to see this thing," breathed Perdita. And so the royal party—two kings, a prince, and an unexpected princess—went to Paulina's home to view the marvelous statue.

"Prepare to see the very imitation of life," warned Paulina, as she drew aside the curtain that covered the statue.

All were amazed, and none more so than Leontes, who was so moved by this lifelike image of his long-dead wife that he stepped forward to touch it.

"Patience!" warned Paulina. "The statue is but newly finished, the color not yet dry."

Leontes continued to stare in amazement. "Would you not deem it breathed?" he asked Polixenes. "Would you not swear those veins pulsed with life?"

"I'll draw the curtain," said Paulina. "It is too disturbing to you to see it."

"No, do not!" cried Leontes.

Paulina turned to him with a strange glint in her eyes. "Either quit the chapel, or prepare for more amazement. If you can behold it, I'll make the statue move, descend, and take you by the hand. But then you'll think I am assisted by wicked powers, which is not so."

"What you can make her do, I am content to see," said the king humbly.

"Then all stand still," ordered Paulina. "Music, awake her!"

From somewhere came strange music. And as it played, Paulina said, "'Tis time; descend; be stone no more; approach; strike all that look upon you with marvel."

For a moment, it seemed as if the world itself were holding its breath. Then the statue stepped from its pedestal.

Leontes cried out in shock and took a step back.

"Do not shun her!" Paulina told the king. "When she was young, you wooed her. Now, in age, is she become the suitor? Present your hand!"

Cautiously the king reached out to her. "She's warm!" he cried. "If this be magic, let it be an art lawful as eating."

Now the statue placed its arms around his neck.

"Make manifest where she has lived, or how been stolen from the dead," demanded Polixenes.

Paulina smiled. "That she is living, were it but told you, should be hooted at like an old tale. But it appears she lives, though yet she speak not. Mark a little while." Turning to Perdita, she said, "Kneel and pray your mother's blessing."

And when the princess did, Hermione—who had been kept in safety and secrecy by Paulina for all these years—spoke at last.

"You gods, look down, and from your sacred vials pour your graces upon my daughter's head!" Taking Perdita's chin in her hand, the queen said, "Tell me, mine own, where has thou been? How found thy father's court? As for me, knowing by Paulina that the oracle gave hope you lived, I have preserved myself to see this very day."

Then there were tears and laughter enough for all, and even more as King Leontes suggested that Camillo, who had long loved Paulina, should be her new husband.

And so there were to be two marriages, that of the prince and the true princess, and that of the faithful servants who had brought them to this place. And it was all so like an old tale that it was told on winter nights long after, in tones of wonder and amazement.

DIAL BOOKS FOR YOUNG READERS

A division of Penguin Young Readers Group • Published by The Penguin Group • Penguin Group (USA) Inc., 375 Hudson Street, New York, NY 10014, U.S.A. • Penguin Group (Canada), 90 Eglinton Avenue East, Suite 700, Toronto, Ontario, Canada M4P 2Y3 (a division of Pearson Penguin Canada Inc.) • Penguin Books Ltd, 80 Strand, London WC2R 0RL, England • Penguin Ireland, 25 St. Stephen's Green, Dublin 2, Ireland (a division of Penguin Books Ltd) • Penguin Group (Australia), 250 Camberwell Road, Camberwell, Victoria 3124, Australia (a division of Pearson Australia Group Pty Ltd) • Penguin Books India Pvt Ltd, 11 Community Centre, Panchsheel Park, New Delhi - 110 017, India • Penguin Group (NZ), Cnr Airborne and Rosedale Roads, Albany, Auckland 1310, New Zealand (a division of Pearson New Zealand Ltd) • Penguin Books (South Africa) (Pty) Ltd, 24 Sturdee Avenue, Rosebank, Johannesburg 2196, South Africa • Penguin Books Ltd, Registered Offices: 80 Strand, London WC2R 0RL, England

Designed by Teresa Kietlinski Dikun
Text set in Goudy
Manufactured in China on acid-free paper

10 9 8 7 6 5 4 3 2 1

Library of Congress Cataloging-in-Publication Data
Coville, Bruce.
William Shakespeare's The winter's tale / adapted by Bruce Coville ; illustrated by LeUyen Pham.
    p.   cm.
ISBN 978-0-8037-2709-0
1. Fathers and daughters—Juvenile fiction. 2. Kings and rulers—Juvenile fiction.
3. Married people—Juvenile fiction. 4. Castaways—Juvenile fiction.
5. Sicily (Italy)—Juvenile fiction. I. Shakespeare, William, 1564–1616.
Winter's tale. II. Pham, LeUyen, ill. III. Title.
PR2878.W5C68 2007
822.3'3—dc22
2006038485

The illustrations in this book were done in watercolor
and gouache on Arches hot-press paper.